OTHER BOOKS BY JOAN AIKEN

WITH QUENTIN BLAKE

The Spiral Stair
Barn Owl Books

Arabel's Raven
Barn Owl Books

Mortimer's Bread Bin
Barn Owl Books

The Winter Sleepwalker
Red Fox

Joan Aiken

Arabel, Mortimer and the Escaped Black Mamba

ILLUSTRATED BY QUENTIN BLAKE

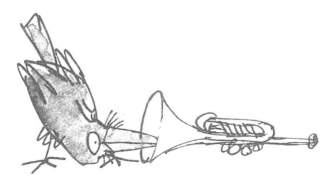

BARN OWL BOOKS

Arabel, Mortimer and the Escaped Black Mamba
was first published as
Arabel and the Escaped Black Mamba
in 1973 by the British Broadcasting Corporation
35 Marylebone High Street, London W1M 4AA
This edition was first published 2002 by Barn Owl Books
157 Fortis Green Road, London N10 3LX
Barn Owl Books are distributed by Frances Lincoln
4 Torriano Mews, Torriano Avenue, London NW5 2RZ

Text copyright © 1973, 2001 Joan Aiken
Illustrations copyright © 1974, 2001 Quentin Blake
The moral right of Joan Aiken to be identified as author and
Quentin Blake as illustrator of this work has been asserted

ISBN 1 903015 24 3

Designed and typeset by Douglas Martin
Printed and bound in Great Britain
by Creative Print and Design Group
Saxon Way, Harmondsworth, Middlesex UB7

For Elise

Chapter One

It was not long after Mortimer the raven took up residence with the Jones family at Number Six, Rainwater Crescent, Rumbury Town, London N.W.3½, that Mr and Mrs Jones received an invitation to the Furriers' Freewheeling Ball at the Assembly Rooms, Rumbury Town.

"What is a Freewheeling Ball?" asked Arabel. Arabel was little and fair, and she didn't go to school yet.

She was eating her breakfast. Mortimer the raven was sitting on her shoulder and peering down into her boiled egg to see if there were any diamonds in it. Mortimer was going through a phase of hoping to find diamonds everywhere.

There were no diamonds in the egg.

"A Freewheeling Ball," said Mr Jones, gloomily putting on his taxi-driving overcoat, "is six hours on your feet after a long hard day's work, with your best suit throttling you, and nothing to eat but potato crisps."

"Kaaark," said Mortimer. He loved potato crisps even better than diamonds.

Arabel imagined them all in their best clothes, pushing a huge freewheeling ball round and round the Assembly Rooms – which were very grand, with red walls and bunches of gold grapes dangling down them.

"You will go to the ball, won't you?" she asked anxiously. "Then Chris Cross can come to babysit."

"I daresay we'll have to," said Mr Jones, looking at the hopeful faces of his wife and daughter. "But mind! If Chris comes he's not to play his guitar after eleven at night. Last time we had trouble from neighbours both sides of the street, right up to the traffic lights."

He kissed his family goodbye, nodded to Mortimer, and went off to drive his taxi.

As he shut the front door, Mortimer fell head-first into Arabel's boiled egg.

"Oh my good gracious Arabel," said Mrs Jones, "why in the name of mystery you can't teach that dratted bird to *balance* I don't know I'm sure. You'd think a creature with wings would have the sense not to lean forward so far he topples over. *Look* at the mess! If I lived to ninety and ended my days in Pernambuco I doubt if I'd ever see anything to equal it!"

"Nevermore," said Mortimer.

As his head was still inside the boiled egg, the word came out muffled.

"Do they have boiled eggs in Pernambuco?" said Arabel.

"How should I know?" said Mrs Jones crossly, clearing away the breakfast dishes. "For gracious' sake, Arabel, put that bird in the bath and run the tap on him, how shall I ever get to the office in time I can't imagine!"

Mrs Jones now worked at Nuggett & Coke, the coal-order office. Arabel and Mortimer loved calling in to see her there; Arabel loved the beautiful blazing fire that always burned in a shiny red stove and Mortimer liked the sample lumps of coke and coal and anthracite in pink plastic bowls on the counter.

Arabel didn't put Mortimer in the bath. She put him, boiled egg and all, on to her red truck and pulled him into the garden. Mortimer never walked if he could ride. And he only flew about twice a year.

"That bird's got an egg on his head," said the milkman, leaving two bottles of milk, two of orange, a dairy cake, a dozen ham-flavoured eggs, and three yoghurts (one rum, one brandy, one worcestershire sauce.)

"Why shouldn't he, if he wants to?" said Arabel.

The milkman had no answer to this, so he went on jangling up the street in his electric trolley.

Presently the egg fell off, Granny came along to look after Arabel and Mortimer, and Mrs Jones went off to work.

Granny made pancakes for lunch and Mortimer helped toss them. Granny did not entirely approve of this, but Arabel said probably there were no pancakes where Mortimer came from and he should have the chance to learn what they were like.

Anyway they got the kitchen floor scrubbed long before Mrs Jones came home.

On the night of the Furriers' Freewheeling Ball, Chris Cross came in to babysit.

Arabel loved Chris. He was not very old, still doing his A-levels at Rumbury Comprehensive, and he had first-rate ideas about how to pass the evening when he came ot the Joneses. He thought of something different and new each time. Last time they had made a Midsummer Pudding, using everything in the kitchen. Also he sang, and played beautiful tunes on his guitar.

"Arabel's to go to bed at half-past eight," said Mr Jones.

"What about Mortimer?" said Chris. He and Mortimer had not met before; they took a careful look at one another.

"He goes to bed when he likes. But he is *not* to sleep in the fridge, *nor* in the airing-cupboard,"

said Mrs Jones putting on her coat. She was wearing a pink satin dress with beads on it.

"Not too noisy on the guitar, now," said Mr Jones.

"I brought my trumpet as well; I'll play that instead if you like," said Chris.

Mr Jones said the guitar would be better.

"And no trumpet after eight *definitely*," he said.

"Supper's in the kitchen," said Mrs Jones. "Mince pies and cheese patties and tomatoes and crisps."

"Kaaaaark," said Mortimer.

"What flavour crisps?" said Arabel.

"Sardine."

Mr and Mrs Jones went off in his taxi, and Chris at once began singing a lullaby:

Morning moon, trespassing down over my
*   skylight's shoulder*
Who asked you to doodle across my deep-seated
*   dream?*
(Basso Bluebells chiming to ice as the night
*   grows colder)*
Be off! Toboggan away on your bothersome
*   beam.*

Arabel loved listening to Chris sing. She stuck her finger in her mouth and sat quite still. Mortimer perched in the coal-scuttle, listening too. He had never heard anybody play the guitar before. He began to get over-excited; he jumped up and down in the coal-scuttle about a hundred times, opening and shutting his wings and shouting, "Nevermore!"

"Doesn't he like the song?" said Chris.

"Oh yes he *does*," said Arabel. "It's just that he's not used to it."

"Maybe we'd better dress up as Paynims and play hide-and-seek."

"How do we dress as Paynims?"

"In towels and helmets."

Arabel used a saucepan as a helmet and

Chris used the pressure-cooker.

"A towel's going to be too big for Mortimer," she said.

"He can have a face-towel. And a sardine tin as a helmet."

Arabel thought a frozen-orange tin would be a better shape.

Mortimer was very amazed at his Paynim costume. They fastened his face-towel on with safety-pins. When it was his turn to hide he climbed into the airing-cupboard (they had opened it to get out the towels). While he was in the cupboard he had a good hunt for diamonds, tearing some sheets and pillow-cases and leaving coaly footprints on Mrs Jones's terylene-lawn nightdress. He did not discover any diamonds. His helmet fell off.

"The cupboard is terribly hot," said Arabel when she found Mortimer. (She had guessed where to look right away, as he was so fond of the airing-cupboard.) "My goodness, Ma went out leaving the immersion heater switched on, the hot-water tank is almost boiling. I had better switch it off." She did so. "Ma will be pleased I thought of doing that," she said.

When it was Chris's turn to hide it took a very long time to find him, as he had packed himself tightly into the laundry-basket and pulled the lid down over his head. He had a book in his pocket, for he had intended to read, but he went to sleep instead.

Arabel hunted for Chris all over the house.

Mortimer, meanwhile, had another idea. He was wondering if there might be any diamonds in the hole inside Chris's guitar. He went off to have a look, leaving Arabel to hunt by herself.

She found her right gumboot, which had been missing for a week, she found a chocolate egg left over from last Easter, she found three pancakes that Mortimer had hidden inside the gramophone and forgotten, but she did not find Chris.

However Mortimer was annoyed to discover that Chris, who never took chances with his beautiful guitar, had placed it and the trumpet on top of the broom cupboard. Since Mortimer never flew if he could possibly avoid it, the guitar was out of his reach.

He looked angrily round the kitchen, with his black eyes that were as bright as privet-berries. The ironing-board stood not very far away.

Mortimer was very strong. He began shoving the ironing-board across the kitchen floor. After five minutes he had it up against the cupboard.

Meanwhile Arabel was still hunting for Chris. She looked in the hat and coat closet under the stairs. There she found a plastic spade left over from Littlehampton last summer and two bottles of champagne which Mr Jones had hidden there as a Christmas surprise for Mrs Jones. No Chris.

Mortimer, in the meantime, was considering, looking at the ironing-board. Then he knocked over the garbage-bucket, tipping out the garbage; he clambered on to a chair, holding the bucket in one claw, and climbed from the chair on to the ironing-board. He put the bucket on the ironing-board, upside-down and got on top of it.

He still could not quite reach the top of the broom cupboard.

Arabel looked for Chris under all the beds. She did not find him but she found one of her blue bedsocks, a ginger biscuit, last Sunday's colour supplement, and a tooth she had lost three weeks before.

Mortimer got down from the garbage bucket and found a square cheese-grater. He made his way back on to the ironing-board, reached up, and balanced the cheese-grater on top of the upside-down bucket; then he clambered carefully up and stood tip-claw on the

cheese-grater's rim.

The bucket rocked about a bit; it was not quite firm on top of the ironing-board.

Still he could not quite reach the top of the broom cupboard.

Arabel looked for Chris under the bath.

She did not find him, but she found all the pearl-handled knives and forks, Mrs Jones's wedding-present fruit-set, that had disappeared shortly after Mortimer came to live in the house. It had been thought that a burglar had taken them.

"Ma *will* be pleased," Arabel said. She carried all the knives and forks to the kitchen wrapped in a fold of her Paynim towel.

When she reached the kitchen the first thing she saw was Mortimer.

He had jammed a milk-bottle into the cheese-grater, which was on top of the bucket, which was upside down on the ironing-board, and he was now very carefully climbing up so as to stand on top of the milk bottle.

The bucket was rocking about a good deal more now, because Mortimer had shifted it sideways as he climbed up and down.

"Oh Mortimer!" said Arabel.

At the sound of her voice Mortimer turned his head and a lot of things happened at once. The bucket fell off the ironing-board, which fell over, the cheese-grater fell off the bucket, the milk bottle (full of milk) fell out of the cheese-grater with Mortimer clinging on to it. The sound made by all these things falling down was quite considerable.

It was like the noise that the dustbin lorry makes when it hoists up its rear end and squashes all the empty boxes and bottles and tins together with a loud, grinding, scrunching clatter.

Chapter Two

The noise made by Mortimer falling off the milk bottle, falling out of the cheese-grater, falling off the bucket, off the overturned ironing-board, woke up Chris Cross, who had been curled up asleep inside the laundry-basket.

He came to see what was happening in the kitchen.

Arabel had a brush and dustpan, and she was sweeping up bits of broken glass. Mortimer was sitting in the fender, looking ruffled. There were splashes of milk all over the floor, and some large puddles too. Quite a few other things were on the floor . . .

"It's a good thing that there were two bottles of milk," Arabel said, remembering that Chris was very fond of milk.

"What happened?" said Chris, yawning.

"I think perhaps Mortimer wanted to look at your guitar."

"Nevermore," said Mortimer, but he didn't sound as if he meant it.

"The guitar had better stay on top of the cupboard for now," said Chris, giving Mortimer a hard look.

"Shall we have supper, as we're all in the kitchen?" said Arabel.

So they had supper, and Mortimer cheered up.

He was not keen on the cheese patties Mrs Jones had made, so Arabel got some frozen braised beef (which he was *very* keen on) out of the fridge. While she was thawing it under the hot tap, Mortimer sat on the cold tap, jumping up and down with impatience and muttering "Nevermore" under his breath. When he was too excited to wait any longer he took the packet from her, whacked a hole in the foil with his big sharp hairy beak and ate the braised beef in a very messy way. Arabel spread the evening paper on the floor and some of the gravy went on that.

Then Mortimer realised, from the scrunching, that the others were eating crisps.

He climbed on the arm of Arabel's chair.

"Do you want some crisps, Mortimer?"

Mortimer jumped up and down. His black eyes shone like the currants on the sticky buns.

Arabel put a handful of crisps on the table in front of him.

Mortimer began eating them as he had the pancakes; he tossed each one in the air and then tried to spear it with his beak before it fell.

All things considered, he was remarkably good at this; much better than Chris and Arabel, who began trying to do it too. But they hadn't got beaks, and had to catch the crisps in their mouths.

Mortimer was spearing his forty-ninth crisp when he hit the milk bottle which was standing on the table beside Chris. It fell on the floor and broke.

"It's lucky we'd drunk half the milk already," said Arabel.

Unfortunately Chris cut his hand while picking up bits of glass.

"Ma says you should always sweep up broken glass with a brush," said Arabel.

"What's the matter, Chris?" He said "I

always faint at the sight of blood." Then he fainted, bumping across the broom cupboard as he went down. His trumpet was dislodged and fell to the floor.

"Oh dear, Mortimer," said Arabel. "It was a pity you knocked over the bottle. I wonder what we had better do now?"

Mortimer paid no attention to Arabel's question. He was studying Chris's trumpet very attentively indeed; first he poked his beak into all the holes; then he stuck his head into the bell; then he went round to the back and peered searchingly into the mouthpiece.

Arabel tried soaking a face-towel in the spilt milk and rubbing it on Chris's forehead. Then she switched on the fan heater to warm his bare feet. Then she put a spoonful of ginger marmalade into his mouth. That made him blink. Mortimer shouted "Nevermore!" in his ear. He blinked again and sat up.

"What happened?" he said.

"You fainted," said Arabel.

"I always faint at the sight of blood," Chris said, looking at his cut finger.

"Well don't faint again," said Arabel. "Here, put this round it." She tore a strip from the face-towel and bandaged Chris's finger with it.

He stood up, swaying a little.

"You ought to have brandy to make you better," said Arabel. "But Pa keeps the brandy in his taxi, in case of lady passengers turning faint."

"I'd rather have milk anyway," said Chris.

However, both bottles of milk were now broken.

"There's a milk-vending machine by the corner shop in the High Street," Chris said. "I'll go out and get some more."

"Ma said you were not to go out and leave me," said Arabel. "I'll come too."

"It's your bedtime."

"No, it isn't, not for five minutes by the kitchen clock. We'd better go right away."

Arabel decided that she did not need a coat, as she was still wearing her Paynim costume, which was a very thick orange towel and her saucepan helmet. She took the front-door key from the nail on the dresser.

"Come on then," said Chris.

"I wonder if we had better take Mortimer too? Ma doesn't like him being left alone in the house."

When they looked round for Mortimer. who had been very quiet for the last few minutes, they found that he had got himself jammed inside Chris's trumpet, face-towel and all. They pulled at his feet, which stuck out, but they couldn't shift him.

"He must have been looking for diamonds in there," said Arabel. "We had better not wait. We can get him out when we come back; I expect if we trickle in a little cooking-oil it will loosen him up."

"Thanks!" said Chris. "Am I supposed to play my trumpet when its full of sunflower oil?"

"Well, it would be better than sump oil," said Arabel. "And you can't play it when it's full of Mortimer."

Luckily Chris's trumpet had a hole in it (he had bought it for fifty pence at the Oxfam shop and stuck a piece of Elastoplast over the hole when he played) so Mortimer was not likely to suffocate. Arabel put him on her red truck, with his feet sticking out of the trumpet, and they walked to the top of Rainwater Crescent, where it joins on to Rumbury High Street at the traffic lights.

It was a dark, windy night. Nobody was about, though they could hear music and voices coming from the disco at the other end of the street.

When they reached the milk machine by the dairy Chris found that he had nothing but a fifty-penny piece and some ones. The machine would take nothing but twenties.

"We could get change at the disco." said Arabel. "It would be silly to go back without any milk now we've come so far."

They walked towards the disco. There was an arcade leading to it, with fruit machines on each side. Arabel had a 20p of her own, so she put it in one of the fruit machines. Some little red balls lit up and rushed about and clanked and shot through holes and bounced on levers and all of a sudden a whole shower of one-penny and five-penny and fifty-penny pieces shot out into the metal cup on the machine's front and a big sign lit up that said: "You are the Winner! You are the next best thing to a millionaire. Why not have another go?"

Mortimer was amazed. By chance, he had been looking that way, through the hole in the trumpet, when all this happened.

"Now we don't need to change your fifty-pence piece, which is a good thing," said Arabel. "We can go back to the milk machine."

So they turned round. Several people had noticed Arabel winning all the money, because the machine made such a commotion.

A couple of sinister-looking men stared at Mortimer. Nothing could be seen of him but his stomach, the tips of his wings and tail, and his two feet with their hairy ankle frills sticking out of the trumpet.

"Look there!" said one of the men, nudging the other. "I bet that's him!"

"I reckon you're right! Barmy sort of disguise, though," said the other man. "Come

on, let's get after them.

They got into a sports car, which was parked illegally on double yellow lines outside the arcade, and followed Arabel and Chris down the street.

Chapter Three

Chris and Arabel walked along Rumbury High Street, pulling Mortimer behind them on Arabel's red truck. When they reached the milk-vending machine, Chris put a 20p piece into its slot. Wheels whirred and levers clanked up and down inside; presently a carton of milk came thumping down into the space in the middle.

This time Mortimer had been watching very intently indeed through the hole in Chris's trumpet. When the carton of milk came into view he said "Kaaark!" several times and began to jump up and down in the red truck, trumpet and all.

"I think he'd like you to put in another one," Arabel said.

This time, when Chris put in two 20p

pieces, for some reason the machine went wild and shot out six cartons of milk.

"My goodness," said Arabel. "We haven't paid for all that. You ought to put in five more."

"I don't know," Chris said, "it isn't our fault if the machine goes crazy."

"We can easily afford to. We've got ten pounds, eight 20p pieces and nine 10 pennies. I've been counting."

So Chris put in five more coins. Nothing happened. The milk machine was tired out.

While Chris and Arabel were piling the seven cartons of milk on the red truck along-side Mortimer, one of the two sinister-looking men in the sport's car (which was now parked not far away) whispered to the other, "That

must be him, mustn't it, Bill?"

The other man nodded.

"The boss is going to be pretty pleased about this, isn't he Sid? We can snatch him back farther up the street where there's no people about."

"Guess they've got him in that trumpet for a disguise."

"Loopy sort of disguise," muttered Bill, easing up the handbrake and letting the car roll slowly along the street.

Arabel, Chris, and Mortimer were now on their way home. But Mortimer was not anxious to go home just yet. He had never come across automatic machines before. He thought they were the most interesting things he had seen in all his life, and he wanted to know all about them.

As the red truck passed Gaskett & Dent, the big garage on the corner, Mortimer peered out through the hole in the trumpet and said "Kaaark!"

Sometimes when he spoke inside the trumpet he accidently blew quite a loud note.

It happened this time, and the sports car swerved sharply across the road.

"What does Mortimer want?" said Chris.

"I think he would like us to put some money in that machine."

"All-night paraffin? What would we want *paraffin* for?"

"We could use it instead of cooking-oil for getting Mortimer out of the trumpet."

"Oh, very well," said Chris. He put in two fifty pence pieces and got a can of paraffin. Mortimer would have liked him to do it again, but Chris thought that one lot of paraffin was quite enough.

"There's a bread machine at the baker's," Arabel said.

"It *must* be past your bedtime by now."

"Well we don't *know* that," Arabel pointed out, "because we haven't got watches. Mortimer would so like to get a loaf from the bread machine."

But at the baker's they had a disappointment. The bread machine was out of order. A sign said so.

"Nevermore," said Mortimer, inside the trumpet.

"Poor thing, he does sound a bit sorry for himself inside there," said Chris. "Tell you what, as we've come so far, we might as well go up to the tube station. There's lots of machines up there."

"Oh yes!" said Arabel.

Rumbury Town Station had recently been modernised inside, after an "accident" to its lifts and escalators. A whole lot of new automatic machines had been installed in the station entrance.

One sold milk, soup, hot chocolate, tea and coffee, black or white, with or without sugar.

Another had apples, pears, and bananas.

Another had paperback books.

Another would polish your shoes.

Another would take a photograph of you looking as if you had seen a ghost.

Another would massage the soles of your feet.

Another would say a cheering poem and hold your hand while it did so.

Another would print your name on a little tin disk.

Another would tell your weight and horoscope.

Another would blow your nose on a clean tissue, if you stuck your nose into a slot, and, as well as that, give you a vitamin C tablet and two mentholated throat sweets, all for two-and-a-half pence.

There was also a useful machine which would give you change for all the others.

Arabel's Great Uncle Arthur was the booking clerk, "Arr," he used to say, "there's that variety of machines at Rumbury Toob now, a man wouldn't need kith nor kin nor wife nor fambly; he could just pass his life in the station and they wondrous machines'd do all he needed. Even his wash he could get done next door at the washeteria; all they don't do for you is to sleep."

Uncle Arthur never needed anyone to do *his* sleeping for him. He was asleep now, with his head pillowed on a pile of fifty-pence tickets, snoring like a brontosaurus.

Mortimer looked around at all the automatic machines with their little glass windows and things for sale all brightly-coloured behind them; his eyes sparkled through the hole in the trumpet like buttons on patent-leather boots.

"Where shall we start?" said Arabel.

Sid and Bill left their car parked illegally outside the station on the double yellow line and strolled up to the entrance. They stood leaning against the wall, looking in.

"Bit public here," said Bill. Sid nodded.

It was at this moment in the Rumbury Town Assembly Rooms, in the middle of the Furriers' Freewheeling Ball, that Mrs Jones suddenly left her partner (Mr Finney the fishmonger), rushed up to Mr Jones, who was gloomily eating potato crisps at the buffet, grabbed his lapel, and said, "Ben, I've just remembered! I left the immersion heater on! Oh my stars, do you suppose the tank will burst and all our sheets and towels will be ruined, and what about Arabel and Mortimer and that boy Chris though I daresay he can take care of himself. Do you suppose they'll be scalded? O my goodness gracious, what a fool I am. What shall we do?"

"It won't burst," said Mr Jones, "But it'll be costing a packet. I'll phone up home and tell Chris to switch it off."

"I'll come to the phone with you," said Mrs Jones, "and make sure Arabel's in bed and everything's all right."

There was a wall telephone in the Assembly Rooms lobby. Mrs Jones dialled his home number but nobody answered. The bell rang and rang.

"Funny," he said. "Maybe I got the wrong number. I'll try again."

He tried again. Still no answer.

"Oh Ben!" said Mrs Jones fearfully. "What can have happened? Can the house have burned down?"

"Don't be silly, Martha. How could the phone ring if the house had burned down? Maybe it's a crossed line. I'll get the exchange to ring them."

He got the exchange. But all they could say was that nobody was answering on Rumbury o-one-one-o.

"Oh Ben! What can have happened? Do you think the boiler did burst? Or perhaps there's been a gas escape and they're all lying unconscious, or masked gunmen are holding them up and they aren't allowed to go to the phone, or there was something deadly in those cheese patties and they're in agony trying to crawl down the stairs, or maybe there's a black mamba escaped from the zoo coiled round the banisters and they can't get by. I've always *said* it was a silly place to have the phone, half-way up the stairs. Oh my gracious, we must go home directly!"

"Don't be silly, we haven't *got* gas, Martha, so how could it escape?"

"From the zoo!" cried Mrs Jones, frantically

waving her cloakroom ticket at the lady who was knitting by the counter. "Oh, please dear, find my coat quick, for a deadly masked mamba has escaped from the gasworks and it's got into the cheese patties and if we don't get home directly there won't be one of them alive to tell the tale."

"What tale?" said the cloakroom lady, rather puzzled, and she was even more puzzled when she looked at the ticket which said *Clean and retexture one pink satin dress.*

"This one, this one then," said Mrs Jones, distractedly fishing out another ticket which said *Rumbury Borough Library Non-Fiction.* "That one, that black coat with the sparkling butterfly brooch on the collar, oh please hurry or I shall pass out with palpitations, I know I shall."

"Why did Mr and Mrs Jones go off so quickly?" asked the cloakroom lady's cousin, Mrs Finney, presently, bringing her some crisps and a glass of sparkling cideringo.

"Oh, Grace, it's awful! One of those deadly cheese mambas has escaped from the telephone exchange and there's gunmen going after it because its breath is like a poison gas and it's in Mr Jones's house coiled round the boiler and everybody's dead and someone just rang from the zoo to tell them to come home."

"My lawks! I'd better tell my hubby, he's a great friend of poor Mr Jones. Perce, Perce, just listen to this: a deadly mamba has escaped from Mr Jones's house and it's in the telephone exchange with a gun and they're trying to gas it out with deadly cheese and all Mr Jones's

family are unconscious inside the boiler and
his house is burnt down."

"Cripes," said Mr Finney, who was a
member of the Auxiliary Fire Brigade. "I'd best
be off, they'll be wanting all the lads at that
rate."

He went towards the entrance, muttering,
"I wonder why they got inside the *boiler*?"

"Take your gas mask!" his wife screeched
after him.

Most of the men at the Furriers' Ball were
glad of the excuse to stream after Mr Finney,
and their wives followed them, all agog to see
what was happening at Number Six, Rainwater
Crescent. A procession of cars started away
from the Assembly Rooms, in pursuit of Mr
Jones's taxi.

Meanwhile Mr and Mrs Jones had arrived at
Number Six.

"At least the *house* is still standing," cried Mrs Jones. "Open the door, Ben, do, I couldn't if I was to be turned into a nutmeg on the spot, my hand's all of a tremble and my saint pancreas is going round and round like a spin dryer."

Mr Jones unlocked the door and they hurried in.

"Arabel," called Mrs Jones, "Arabel, dearie, where are you? It's Mum and Dad come home to save you!"

No answer.

Chapter Four

Mrs Jones rushed to the kitchen, where the light was on, and screamed.

"Oh my dear cats alive, look! Ben! Oh, whatever has been going on? Broken glass everywhere – blood – milk – towels – what's that guitar doing up on top of the cupboard? Cheese-grater on the floor, crisps everywhere, pressure-cooker lid in the laundry-basket, a whole *gang* of mambas must have been in! Ben! This house has been ransacked!"

Even Mr Jones was obliged to admit that it looked as if there had been a struggle.

"I'd best call the police," he said unhappily, when he had been all over the house and had made sure that neither Arabel, nor Mortimer, nor Chris was anywhere in it. "There's been something funny going on in the airing-cupboard too; one thing, the intruders seem to have had the sense to turn off the immersion heater. Not before time. The water's boiling."

"Oh, how can you talk about immersion heaters when my child's been gagged and tied up in a lot of sheets and towels," lamented Mrs Jones. "Kidnapped, that's what they've been, by a gang of gorillas that live in the River Jordan. Oh Ben! We'll never set eyes on them again. My little Arabel! And Mortimer! Oh why did I ever say a cross word about him? To think I'll never see him digging for diamonds in the coal-scuttle any more!"

"Oh come, Martha, things may not be as bad as that," said Mr Jones doubtfully. "Let's see what the police say, anyway." He went to the phone and dialled 999.

"Send back a lock of hair in a matchbox, they will," wept Mrs Jones. "Or a claw, maybe! Heart of gold that bird had at bottom; just a rough diamond with feathers on he was. Many's the time I've seen him look at me as though he'd have *liked* to think a kind thought if his nature would have let him."

"I want the police," said Mr Jones into the telephone.

But at that moment the police, three of them, came through the front door, which was open.

It was Sergeant Pike, who had met Mr Jones not long before, when Mortimer was helpful in catching the Cash-and-Carat boys. With the sergeant there were also two constables.

"Evening, Mr J.," said the sergeant "Having a little trouble, are you? Someone up the town reported you've an escaped snake in the house, is that right?"

"Snake? Who said anything about a snake?"

Mr Jones was puzzled. "No, it's my daughter and our raven Mortimer and the babysitter who seem to have been overpowered and kidnapped, sergeant. They aren't anywhere in the house. You can see there's been quite a fight here. Look at this blood on the floor."

"Carried off to Swanee Arabia they've been by a band of gorillas," sobbed Mrs Jones. "Blown up in a hijacked plane they'll be, any minute now, in that nasty desert."

"That's human blood on the floor, that is," said one of the constables, as if no one had noticed it before.

"You can see there's bin a struggle. Someone tore a strip off that towel."

"For a gag, likely."

"The guitar got tossed up on top of the cupboard in the roughhouse."

"The garbage bin got kicked over in the scrimmage."

"The ironing-board was upset in the ruckus."

"Someone bashed someone's head with a milk bottle."

"And another bloke took and bashed him back with another bottle."

"And collared him when he was down and scraped him with the cheese-grater."

"That'll be Grievous Bodily Harm, shouldn't wonder."

"Cheese-grater," said the sergeant thoughtfully, "Wasn't there something about some poisoned cheese patties talked of up the town?"

Just at that moment there was a tremendous clanging of bells and the fire-engine drew up outside.

"Can we help?" called Mr Finney, who, with his mates, had got into auxiliary fire uniform.

They all rushed into the house, still hastily swallowing down the last of the sandwiches they had snatched up from the buffet at the Assembly Rooms, waving their fire-axes and looking eagerly for black mambos.

"I dunno," said the sergeant. "Why are you all wearing gas masks?"

"Someone said a tank full of deadly mambas had exploded and there was a lot of gas about."

Now all the ladies from the Furriers' Ball turned up, looking like the chorus of a play about Ancient Egypt.

"We've brought hot tea and blankets," cried Mrs Finney. "Where's all the injured persons?"

"Strewth," said the sergeant. "How am I expected to get anything done, with all this shower?"

People swarmed all over the house, looking at the mess. Every room was filled with ladies, blankets, firemen, axes.

"Do you find you can get your sink *really* clean with Dizz, dear?" said Mrs Finney to Mrs

Jones. "I always find Swoosh is ever so much better."

"Fancy you still having those old-fashioned plastic curtains in your kitchen! Give it ever such an old-world look, don't they? My Hubby *made* me change to blinds, much more modern and labour-saving and Continental –"

"Haven't you ever thought of getting a sink rubbish disposal unit, dear?"

"I have lost my beloved daughter and my greatly esteemed raven," said Mrs Jones with dignity, "and I should be obliged if you would kindly leave me alone with my trouble."

"Yes, why don't all you ladies go and have a hunt up and down the street, see if you can lay eyes on the little girl," said the sergeant, "or one of these here pistol-packing mambas I hear talk of. Be off, buzz along, clear out, that's right, let's have a bit of peace and quiet round here, can we?"

"Suppose we meet the mambas, what shall we do?"

"It isn't mambas, it's gorillas," wailed Mrs Jones.

"Do not attempt to engage them in combat but inform the police," said Sergeant Pike. "If you patrol the High Street in half-dozens I daresay you'll be safe enough."

He shoved the reluctant ladies out of the house.

"What about us?" said Finney hopefully, looking about for something to bash with his fireman's axe. In his gas mask he looked like some creature that had climbed up out of the deep, deep sea.

"You cruise up and down the High Street in your fire-engine and assist the ladies in their enquiries," instructed Sergeant Pike and shoved Mr Finney out too. "Now, Mr and Mrs Jones, if you'll just accompany me up to the station and make a statement, perhaps this case can then proceed in a proper and orderly manner."

"Why go to the tube station? Oh my stars, why can't we make a statement here when all the time my Arabel's lying bound and gagged on some railway line in the desert with all the Arabian Knights of the Round Table ready to chop her in half if she moves hand or foot?"

P. C. Smith and P. C. Brown, who had been searching the house, came to report.

"Someone's been incarcerated in the airing-cupboard," P. C. Smith said. "There's an empty orange-juice tin there, also a ginger biscuit, a chocolate egg, and three battered pancakes."

"Ah," said Sergeant Pike, "that proves it was a carefully planned and premeditated job. The intruder must have been hiding in the airing-cupboard before you left for the Ball, Mr Jones, waiting till you were out of the house. He may have been there for days, even."

"He must have been ever so small then," wept Mrs Jones, for *I* never saw him when I turned the heater on for Arabel's bath. Oh my goodness, it must have been one of those wicked, fiendish little dwarfs capable of super-human strength like Mr Quilp in *Old Curiosity Shop* or the hunchback of the Aswan Dam. To think he's been in the house all this time. Oh my poor nerves!"

"Let's get up to the station for pete's sake," said Sergeant Piuke, who began to feel he was losing his grip on the case. "Do you want to come in the police car or will you follow in your taxi?"

"We'll follow," said Mr Jones.

After the police had left Mr Jones carefully locked the house, and he and Mr Jones followed in his taxi.

But they got left behind almost at once, because whenever Mrs Jones laid eyes on a group of searching ladies in the street she made her husband slow down while she put her head out of the window and shouted: "It's not gorillas after all, it's those fiendish little dwarf Arabian Knights with curved swords that go round cutting cushions in half in old curiosity shops."

Mr Halliwell, the bank manager, a keen do-it-yourself man, was mobbed by a group of determined ladies who thought that the forty yards of patent draft excluder which he was carrying home draped round his neck was a ferocious black mamba busily dragging him off to its lair.

Luckily Mr and Mrs Jones arrived in the taxi at this point; Mr Jones drove slowly through the group, honking his horn, and the ladies were obliged to scatter out of the road. Mr Halliwell managed to escape down a side road before they caught him again.

Meanwhile down at the Assembly Rooms, a Jones Family Disaster Fund had been started. Already the collection had reached nine pounds, fifty-three pence, one of a pair of diamond cufflinks and half a chicken sandwich.

"Now, Mrs Jones," said the superintendant, when the Joneses arrived at the police station, "you say you have reason to believe that your daughter Arabel has been kidnapped?"

"*And* our raven Mortimer and the babysitter, Chris Cross."

"We'll take them one at a time, please. Now, Mrs Jones, what was your daughter Arabel doing when you saw her last?"

Mrs Jones blushed pink. "Oh, I couldn't tell you that," she began.

"Come, come, Mrs Jones, this is no time for reticence. Provided your daughter was not committing a misdemeanour – or even if she *was* –"

"It's nothing like that," Mr Jones interrupted crossly. "When last seen my daughter Arabel had a pressure-can full of deodorant talcum powder and she was squirting it over my socks. It was her mother's idea."

"And did you then proceed to put on those socks?"

"No, I left them in the bath."

One of the constables nodded. "There was a pair of socks in the bath covered with heavily scented white powder. I thought they might have been used for drugging someone so I brought them along."

"And what was Mortimer the raven doing when last seen?"

"He had just stepped into the pressure can's line of fire and been squirted all over with deodorant powder. He was rather annoyed about it. Before that he had been throwing small pellets of paper out of the window."

"He might have been sending messages to his accomplices?"

Mr Mortimer shook his head. "Not Mortimer."

"Why not?"

"No accomplice could stand Mortimer's ways.

"And the babysitter? What was he doing?"

"He was playing his guitar and singing a song about a two-gun two-timing kid from Kansas."

"That's very suspicious," said the superindendant. "Definite hint of kidnapping there. Depend on it, that babysitter was in the plot!"

Chapter Five

Meanwhile, up at the tube station, Arabel,
Mortimer and Chris had been having a
wonderful time. Mortimer, jumping up and
down in frantic excitement inside his trumpet,
had watched while they put coins into every
single machine, one by one. On the red truck,
as well as seven cartons of milk and the
paraffin, they now had a packet of wine gums,
two bars of chocolate, one of nuts and raisins,
some cigarettes, a ham sandwich, four empty
cups (one chocolate, one milk, one coffee, one
soup), an apple, a pear, a banana, a copy of a
paperback book called *Death in the Desert*, a
make-it-yourself gramophone record of Chris
singing his song about the moon, a meat pie, an
identity disk with Mortimer's name and
address printed on it, a photograph of Arabel

with Mortimer in his trumpet on her shoulder,
a card saying that Chris weighed ten stone and
would marry a dark girl and have six children,
a Vitamin C tablet, and two mentholated throat
sweets. Also Arabel had had her nose blown
and Mortimer his feet massaged, which had
astonished him very much indeed.

"That's all," said Arabel regretfully, when
they had put the mentholated throat sweets
into an empty cup which had held tomato
soup. "Could we start again?"

"No, we ought to go home," said Chris. "It
must be your bedtime by now."

"We could wake Uncle Arthur and ask him
the time in case it isn't."

"No, don't lets, he looks so peaceful. Come on, we can make some more hot chocolate when we get back, now we've got all this milk."

They pulled Mortimer out of the tube station on his truck and started down the hill.

The two men who had been waiting got back into their car and followed slowly.

But Mortimer, when he found that the evening's entertainment was finished, became very despondent. He began to grumble inside the trumpet, and to mutter, and flap his wings, or try to, and kick the can of paraffin, and shout "Nevermore!" in a loud, angry voice.

"He's upset because *he* didn't have the chance to put any money in a machine," said Arabel.

"He shouldn't have got inside my trumpet then, should he?"

"If we could only get it off him," said Arabel, "we could turn down Lykewake Lane and go home that way. There's a draper's shop there that has a machine outside that you put twopence in and it sews on a button while you wait."

"Who wants a button sewn on?"

"Mortimer might like one on his face towel."

"Oh all right."

So they turned down Lykewake Lane (just missing one of the groups of ladies and the fire-engine cruising along the High Street), and the two men followed along behind in their car.

When they came to the draper's shop, which was called Cotton & Button, Arabel said: "Mortimer, will you stop shouting Nevermore and listen? We are going to pull the trumpet off you – if we can – and then you can put two pence in this machine for it to sew on a button."

Silence from inside the trumpet while Mortimer thought about this.

"Do you think we really ought to pour paraffin on him?" said Chris. "Suppose it's bad for him? And it will make my trumpet smell terrible?"

"Well," said Arabel, "if you don't think we ought, Pa told me there's an Italian grocer's shop in Highgate that has an olive oil machine."

"I'm not walking all the way over to Highgate."

"In that case we'll have to use the paraffin," said Arabel. "Mortimer. We are going to turn you upside down and pour a little paraffin into the trumpet so as to loosen you and pull you out. We are doing this for your good. Will you please try not to struggle?"

Silence.

Arabel picked up the trumpet and turned it upside down. Chris picked up the paraffin container.

At this moment the two men who had been following got out of their car and came quietly up beside them. Both were holding guns.

"Give us that bird – he's valuable – come on hand him over!"

"We know he's valuable," said Arabel. "He's my raven, Mortimer."

"How are we going to get him out if we don't pour paraffin?" said Chris.

"Why are you holding guns?" said Arabel. "You look rather silly."

"That bird's no raven. That bird is a

valuable mynah bird, the property of Slick Sim Symington, the Soho property millionaire. That bird was captured last week by a rival gang – by a rival establishment – and it is our intention to get possession of him again. So hand him over."

"Hand over Mortimer?" said Arabel. "Not likely! Why, he's my very own raven, he loves me, and he certainly is not a minor bird, whatever they are."

"We'll soon see about that," said Bill. Putting his gun down on the red truck he grabbed hold of the trumpet with both hands while Sid, putting down *his* gun, grabbed Mortimer's feet.

There was a short, sharp struggle, during which it was hard to see what was going on. Then the scene cleared, to show Mortimer sitting on Arabel's shoulder. His face-towel had come off. The trumpet was on the ground. The two men were both bleeding freely from a number of wounds.

"Nevermore," said Mortimer.

"*I'll* say it's nevermore," said Bill. "That's no mynah bird."

"What a Turk," said Sid. "Lucky he missed my jugular. You're right, miss, he's a raven, and all I can say is, I wish you joy of the black brute."

"Very sorry you were troubled," said Bill. "Here, come on Sid, let's get over to Rumbury Central *quick*, and have us some anti-tetanus injections before we're rolling around like the exhibits in one of those kinetic shows."

They jumped into their car and roared off, just missing the fire-engine as they turned into the High Street.

"Hey," shouted Arabel, "you've left your guns behind.

But it was too late, they had gone.

"Oh well," said Arabel, "perhaps they'll call in for the guns tomorrow. Anyway, Mortimer, now you can sew on some buttons. We've got eighteen twopences left."

So Mortimer, jumping up and down with

satisfaction and enthusiasm, put eighteen twopences into the slot machine and it sewed seventeen buttons on to the face-towel. (One of the twopences turned out to be an old half-penny with a hole in it.)

Then they went home and let themselves in with Arabel's key. They tidied up the kitchen and the airing-cupboard. Chris mopped the floor. Then he made a saucepan full of hot chocolate while Arabel had a bath, and he brought her a mugful in bed, and she drank it.

Then she had to get out of bed again to brush her teeth. Then she went to sleep.

Mortimer had already gone to sleep in the coal-scuttle. He was tired out.

Chris put all the cartons of milk, except the

one they had used for chocolate, into the
fridge, with the ham sandwich, the meat pie,
the wine gums, the chocolate bars and the
throat tablets; he put the cigarettes, apple and
pear, and paperback book on to the dresser,
and the paraffin outside in the shed. He ate the
nuts and raisins and the banana.

He did not know what to do with the guns,
so he left them on Arabel's red truck.

Then he put his do-it-yourself record on the gramophone and sat down to listen.

*Morning moon, trespassing down, over my
    skylight's shoulder
Who asked you to doodle across my deep-seated
    dream?*

At that moment the front door burst open

and in rushed Mr and Mrs Jones, police, firemen, and a lot of ladies with blankets and thermos flasks of tea.

"Arabel? Oh, where's my child?" cried Mrs Jones, when she saw Chris.

"Where's the gorillas?" asked Mrs Finney.

"And the mambas?" asked Mr Finney.

"And this gang of dwarf Arabian hunchbacks?" said Sergeant Pike?

"Arabel? Why she's asleep in bed," said Chris, puzzled. "Where else would she be? You're back early, aren't you?"

Mrs Jones ran up the stairs.

Sure enough, there was Arabel, asleep in

bed.

"What about Mortimer?"

"He's asleep in the coal-scuttle."

There was a long, long silence while everybody gazed about at the tidy kitchen.

At length Mr Jones said, "What's that guitar doing up on top of the broom cupboard?"

"I put it there to be out of Mortimer's reach," said Chris. "He wanted to look for diamonds in it."

"He does do that sometimes," said Mr Jones, nodding.

After another long silence, Sergeant Pike said, "If you ask *me*, everybody in this room has been suffering from one o' them mass delusions. If you ask *me,* we'd better all forget about this evening's occurrences and go home to bed."

Nobody disagreed. They all filed silently out of Mrs Jones's kitchen and out of the house.

Mr Finney muttered, maybe there *was* an escape of gas and it sort of affected everybody's mind. Or maybe it was food poisoning. Those crisps up the Assembly Rooms didn't taste very fresh to me."

Mr and Mrs Jones paid Chris his babysitting fee and he went home. Then they went to bed. They were almost as tired as Mortimer.

Next day, when Mr Jones had gone off to drive his taxi, Mrs Jones said to Arabel, "What's all this milk doing in the fridge, and this meat pie and ham sandwich?"

"Did you go out after your bedtime?"

"No, it was twenty-five past eight. We got some other things from automatic machines too. Those cigarettes are a present for Pa, and that book is a present for you."

Mrs Jones looked at the paperback called *Death in the Desert.* It had a picture of a person tied to a railway line.

"Thank you, dearie. I'll read it sometime when I'm not busy," she said, and put it on a high shelf of the dresser. Then she said, "Where did those toy guns come from?"

"I don't think they are toys," said Arabel. "They belong to two men, I think they were miners, who thought Mortimer was an escaped miner's bird. But they soon saw he wasn't."

"Funny," said Mrs Jones. But I believe I did hear they used birds in the mines to smell if there's a gas escape. I didn't know miners had to carry guns, though. Oh well, I daresay they'll come back for them."

She put the guns on another high shelf.

For a long time after that, people in Rumbury Town talked about the evening when

the deadly black mamba escaped from the
gasworks.

Mrs Jones was so pleased to have back her
pearl-handled knives and forks that she forgave
Arabel for the seventeen buttons sewn on the
face-towel and the strip torn of it.

Mortimer slept in the coal-scuttle for
seventeen hours. Then he woke up and began
digging for diamonds. He threw all the coal out
on to the kitchen hearth-rug, lump by lump.

But he did not find any diamonds in the
coal-scuttle.

THE SPIRAL STAIR
By Joan Aiken and Quentin Blake

Rare animal thieves are around and only Arabel and her raven Mortimer (with a little help from Noah the Boa) can foil their wicked plans.

Huge fun at the zoo as three giraffes struggle for doughnuts and Mortimer tries to get more than his fair share.

ISBN 1-903015-07-3 £3.99

ARABEL'S RAVEN
By Joan Aiken and Quentin Blake

The first adventure of Arabel and her raven Mortimer. Mr Jones nearly runs the raven over while driving his cab. Being a kind man Mr Jones takes the raven home and Arabel his daughter insistes that the raven stay and be her best friend. From thast day oin there is no peace in the Jones house or Rumbury Town. Still when it comes to dealing with jewel thieves Mortimer has his uses.

ISBN 1-903015-14-6 £3.99

MORTIMER'S BREAD BIN
By Joan Aiken and Quentin Blake

Mortimer the raven is determined to sleep in the bread bin but Mrs Jones is equally determined that he won't After a series of hair-raising adventures at a roller skating rink Mrs Jones is happy to give in. Particvularly when Mortimer helps poor sick Arabel to recover in hospital.

More hilarious fun from Arabel and Mortimer.

ISBN 1-903015-15-4 £3.99

THE BOY WHO SPROUTED ANTLERS
by John Yeoman and Quentin Blake

When Billy Dexter is challenged to grow horns, he doesn't think he can do it. However, the next morning, there they are, two little horns pushing through and as the days go on Billy develops the most splendid head of antlers ever. Everyone gets used to them, Billy and his friends, his parents, even his teacher and the head, but will the antlers stay for ever or will Billy find a way to get rid of them?

A charming story about daring to be different.

ISBN 1-903015-19-7 £3.99